WORKING HARD WITH THE RESCUE HELICOPTER

Written by Cynthia Benjamin
Illustrated by Steven James Petruccio

SCHOLASTIC INC.
New York   Toronto   London   Auckland   Sydney

Look for these other books about Tonka trucks:

Working Hard with the Busy Fire Truck

Working Hard with the Mighty Dump Truck

Working Hard with the Mighty Loader

Working Hard with the Mighty Mixer

Building the New School

Fire Truck to the Rescue

Working Hard with the Mighty Tractor Trailer and Bulldozer

Big City Dump Truck

Big Farm Tractor

ISBN 0-590-13449-3

TONKA® and TONKA® logo are trademarks of Hasbro, Inc.
Used with permission.
Copyright © 1997 by Hasbro, Inc. All rights reserved.
Published by Scholastic Inc.

15   16   17   18   19   20

Printed in the U.S.A.   23

First printing, May 1997

I'm a helicopter pilot. Every day I fly my rescue helicopter to many different places. Spend a day with me and my copilot and see how we help people.

I make sure my helicopter is ready to fly. Before taking off, I check all the controls in the cockpit. The lever on my left makes the helicopter go straight up or down. The one in front of me makes the helicopter fly in different directions — forward, backward, even sideways!

My rescue helicopter is an amazing flying machine!
It can stay in one place when it's high in the air.
When the helicopter hovers this way, it looks like a giant bird.
I take off straight up in the air.

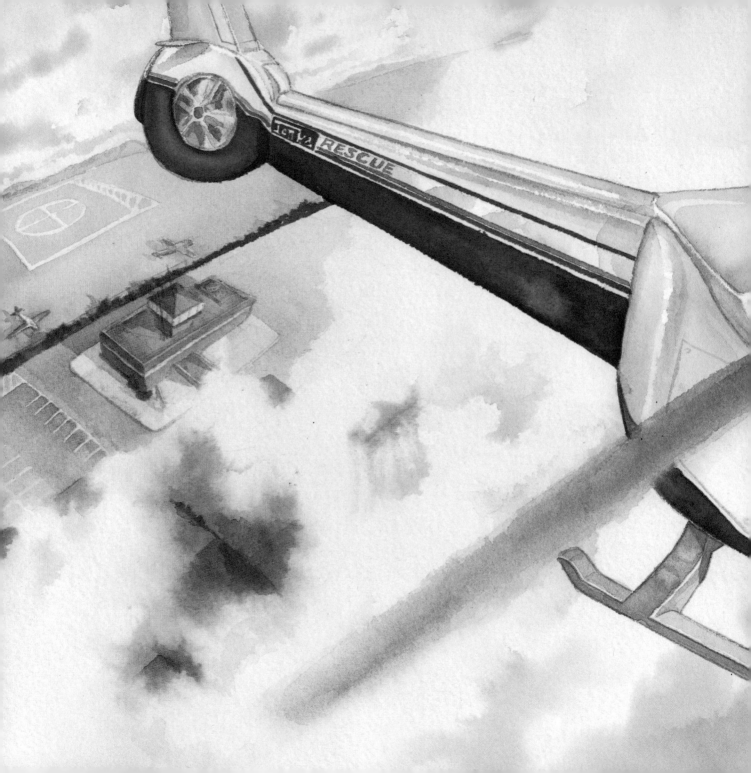

A powerful engine turns the long rotor blades. When they spin around, the helicopter climbs high in the air and flies.
The rotor blades make a whirring sound. Some nicknames for a helicopter are "whirlybird" and "eggbeater."

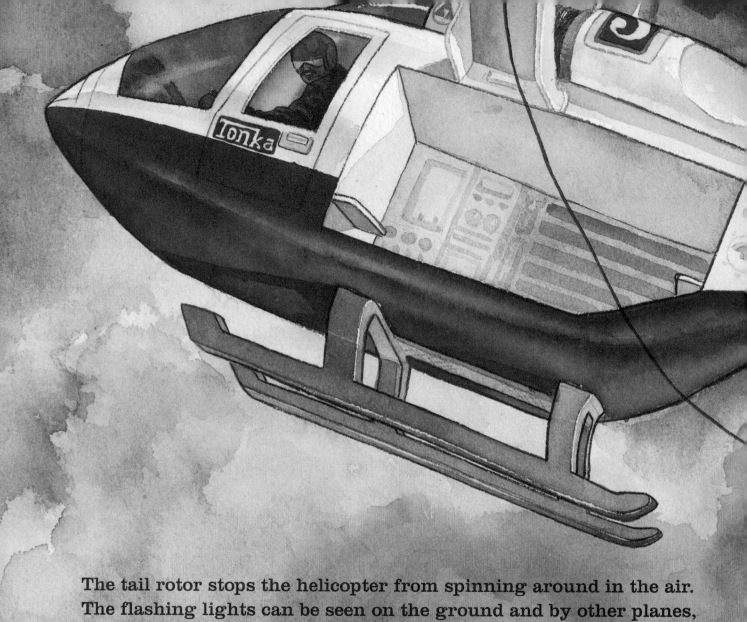

The tail rotor stops the helicopter from spinning around in the air.
The flashing lights can be seen on the ground and by other planes,
too. The long skids on the bottom are used when I land the
helicopter. The gurney safely holds the people that I rescue.
The winch raises and lowers the gurney.

The dispatcher is calling me
on my radio. Uh, oh! There's
a big fire in that skyscraper
on Green Street. My helicopter
lights flash! The siren roars!
Over and out. I'm on my way.

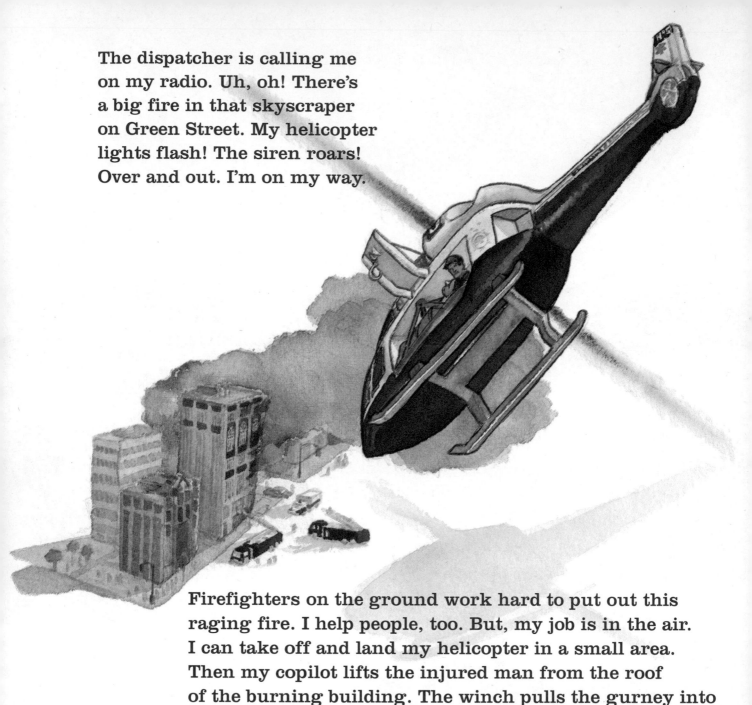

Firefighters on the ground work hard to put out this
raging fire. I help people, too. But, my job is in the air.
I can take off and land my helicopter in a small area.
Then my copilot lifts the injured man from the roof
of the burning building. The winch pulls the gurney into
the helicopter. We're on our way to the nearest hospital.

I land the rescue helicopter on the hospital roof.
Now the injured man can get the medical treatment he needs.
A few minutes later, I'm in the air again.

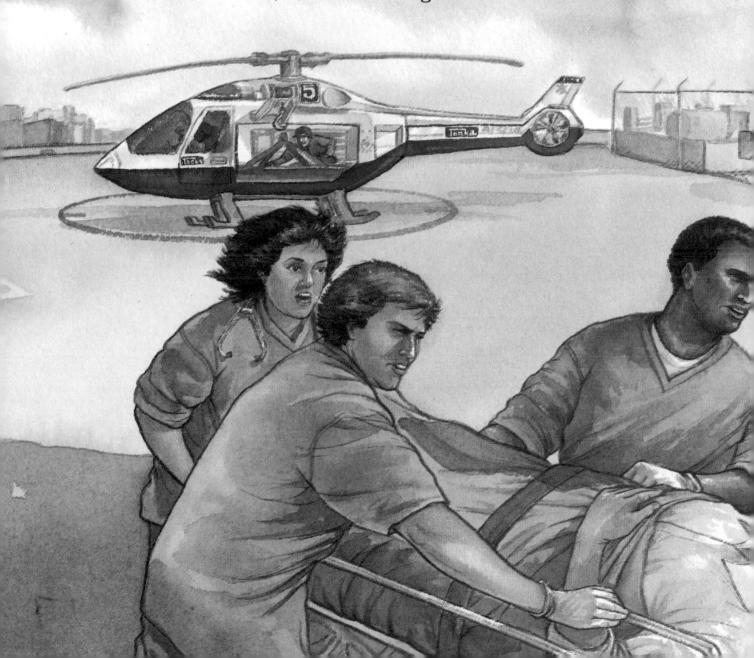

My helicopter is perfect for rescuing people who are in trouble.
That woman has fallen from the deck of her ship.
I hover in the air above the rough sea to save her.

After pulling her from the water, I fly her to the shore.

The harbor patrol
is waiting for us.

After saying good-bye to the harbor patrol,
I fly straight up in the air.
My rescue helicopter can fly 200 miles per hour!

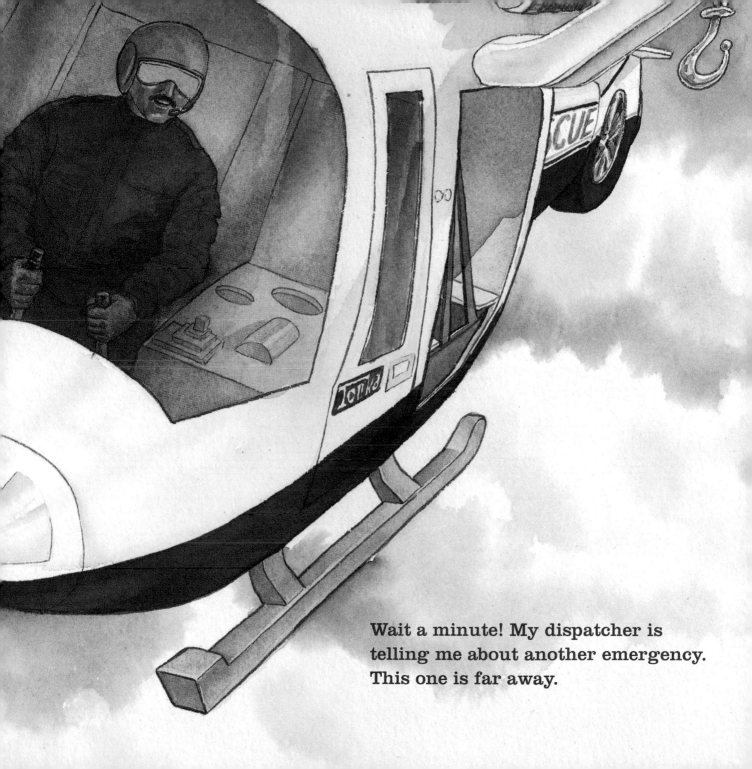

Wait a minute! My dispatcher is telling me about another emergency. This one is far away.

A hurricane destroyed the bridge leading to this small town. The fallen trees have blocked the major roads. Although a car or ambulance can't get through, my rescue helicopter can.

Since I carry food, medicine, and other supplies,
I can drop them to the people who need them
in this emergency.

The fierce storm also caused a nearby river to overflow its banks. I see someone stranded on that roof.

The little boy is safe inside the strong harness of the gurney.

I take a break and return to the heliport.
The crew refuels the helicopter.
The powerful engine uses kerosene fuel.

Now it's time to go back to work.
My rescue helicopter flies over the tall
mountains that surround the city.

That man injured himself
while he was skiing down the mountain.
My rescue helicopter is like a flying ambulance.
I'll take the injured skier to a nearby hospital.

I have one more stop to make.
Far out at sea, the crew on that oil rig
is working hard. They depend on the
rescue helicopter to bring supplies to them.

There's a space for me to land on the oil rig
called a helideck. It's getting foggy and windy now.
Landing safely will be a little tricky because of the weather.
But I make it and deliver their supplies.

It's been a long day. Now it's time to head home.

I leave my helicopter at the heliport for the night.
I'm on my way to celebrate a special day with
my family.

I'm just in time for my daughter's birthday party!